For George Williams

First published 2009 by Walker Books Ltd
87 Vauxhall Walk, London SE11 5HJ

This edition published 2012

2 4 6 8 10 9 7 5 3 1

This book has been typeset in Gill Sans MT Schoolbook

Printed in China

British Library Cataloguing in Publication Data:
a catalogue record for this book is available
from the British Library

ISBN 978-1-4063-4047-1

www.walker.co.uk

Tilly and
her friends
all live
together in
a little yellow
house...

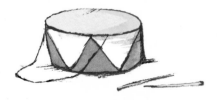

Goodnight
Tiptoe

Polly Dunbar

WALKER BOOKS
AND SUBSIDIARIES
LONDON · BOSTON · SYDNEY · AUCKLAND

Hector yawned.

Tilly yawned.

Everybody

yawned! Everybody except Tiptoe.

"It's time
for bed,"
said Hector,
snuggling up.

Tilly gave Tiptoe a kiss goodnight.
"I'm not sleepy,"
he said.

Tilly helped put Pru's rollers in.
"Look who's not in bed," said Pru.

"I'm still not sleepy," said Tiptoe. "I don't want to go to bed."

"You can stay up while I clean
Doodle's teeth," said Tilly.
"Then it's back to bed."

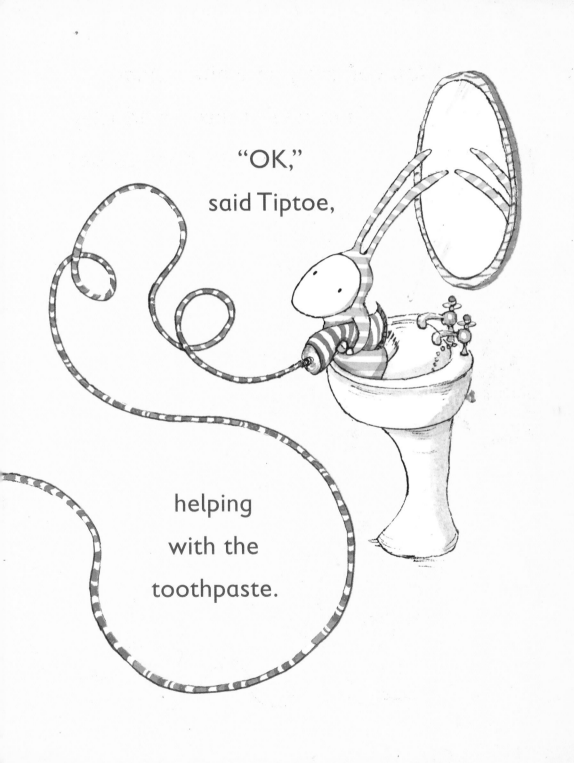

"OK,"
said Tiptoe,

helping
with the
toothpaste.

"Now it **really** is
time for bed," said Tilly.
She sang a lovely lullaby.

TRA LA LA LA

When Tilly
had settled Tiptoe
down again,
she helped Tumpty
with his bath.

"I want a story,"

said Tiptoe.

So Tilly read
a bedtime
story.

Everybody felt very, very, sleepy.

Even Tiptoe closed his eyes.

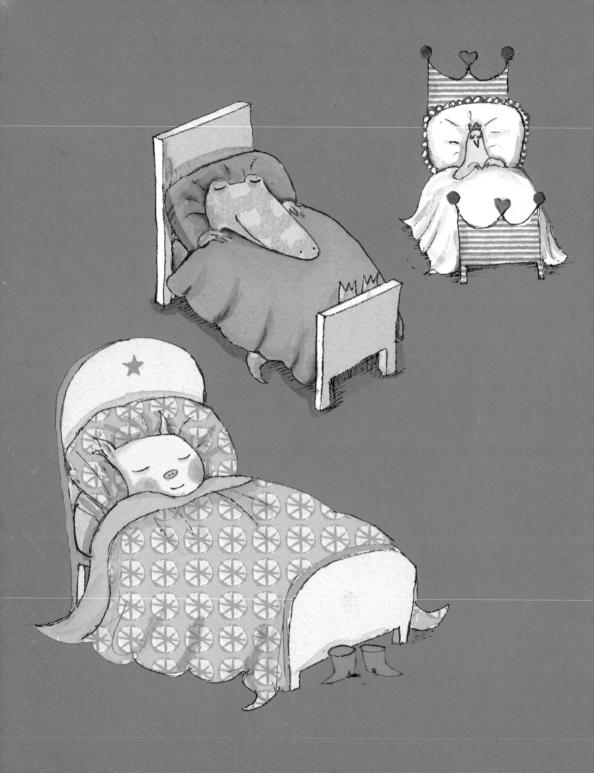

"Sssssshhhh!" whispered Tilly.

"I feel sleepy now,"
said Tilly.
"It must be my bedtime too."
She cleaned her teeth
all by herself.

Tilly got into bed
all by herself.
"Who's going to tuck **me** in?"
she said.
"Who's going to kiss
me goodnight?"

"I am!"

said

Tiptoe.

Goodnight! x

Polly Dunbar

Polly Dunbar is one of today's most exciting young author-illustrators, her warm and witty books captivating children the world over.

Polly based the Tilly and Friends stories on her own experience of sharing a house with friends. Tilly, Hector, Tumpty, Doodle, Tiptoe and Pru are all very different and they don't always get on. But in the little yellow house, full of love and laughter, no one can be sad or cross for long!

ISBN 978-1-4063-4024-2

ISBN 978-1-4063-4048-8

ISBN 978-1-4063-4049-5

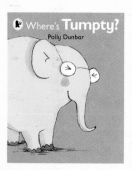

ISBN 978-1-4063-4045-7

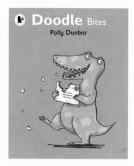

ISBN 978-1-4063-4046-4

ISBN 978-1-4063-4047-1

"Nobody can draw anything more instantly loveable than one of Dunbar's characters."
Independent on Sunday

Available from all good booksellers

www.walker.co.uk